And there she would wait very quietly until
somebody came along . . .

And when that somebody did, she would tiptoe up behind them, open her mouth wide and shout . . .

"BOO!"

And do you know why Little Miss Scary did this?

For fun.

You see, she loved to scare people more than anything else in the world.

And she was very good at it.

She scared them stiff.

"BOO!"

She scared them out of their wits.

"BOO!"

She even scared them right out of their socks.

"BOO!"

About a week ago, Mr Noisy went to see his friend Mr Jelly.

Mr Noisy was worried because he hadn't heard from his friend for ages.

When he got to Mr Jelly's house, he knocked on the door.

Spookily, the door swung open by itself.

"Hello," called Mr Noisy as softly as he could, which for you or I would have been a shout.

Then he heard a chattering noise coming from the bedroom.

Mr Noisy found Mr Jelly hiding under his bed, his teeth chattering in fear.

"Whatever's the . . . " began Mr Noisy, and then remembered himself. "Whatever's the matter, Mr Jelly?"

"It's . . . it's . . . L-L-Little Miss S-S-Scary," chattered Mr Jelly, trembling in fear. "Sh-sh-she keeps jumping out and shouting 'b-b-b-boo' at me."

Mr Noisy made Mr Jelly a cup of tea, calmed him down and told him what they were going to do.

Just as it was getting dark, they hid behind a bush beside the lane that led up to Mr Jelly's house.

They waited until they saw Little Miss Scary's shadowy figure creeping past them.

Then Mr Noisy and Mr Jelly crept out from their hiding place, tiptoed up behind Little Miss Scary and, at the top of their voices, shouted . . .

"BOO!"

Now, the top of Mr Noisy's voice is a very loud place indeed.

So loud that Little Miss Scary leapt five feet in the air and when she came down she ran for her life.

She didn't stop running until she was hidden under her bed.

In her bedroom.

In Spooky Cottage.

At the top of the mountain.

"I don't think you'll be seeing much of her for a long while, Mr Jelly," chuckled Mr Noisy. "Mr Jelly? Mr Jelly . . .?"

But there was no sign of Mr Jelly either.

Mr Noisy chuckled again and walked back to
Mr Jelly's house. To have a look under Mr Jelly's bed!

Fantastic offers for Little Miss fans!

Collect all your Mr. Men or Little Miss books in these superb durable collectors' cases!
Only £5.99 inc. postage and packing, these wipe-clean, hard-wearing cases will give all your Mr. Men or Little Miss books a beautiful new home!

Keep track of your collection with this giant-sized double-sided Mr. Men and Little Miss Collectors' poster.
Collect 6 tokens and we will send you a brilliant giant-sized double-sided collectors' poster! Simply tape a £1 coin to cover postage and packaging in the space provided and fill out the form overleaf.

STICK £1 COIN HERE
(for poster only)

Only need a few Little Miss or Mr. Men to complete your set? You can order any of the titles on the back of the books from our Mr. Men order line on 0870 787 1724. Orders should be delivered between 5 and 7 working days.

--- **TO BE COMPLETED BY AN ADULT** ---

To apply for any of these great offers, ask an adult to complete the details below and send this whole page with the appropriate payment and tokens, to: MR. MEN CLASSIC OFFER, PO BOX 715, HORSHAM RH12 5WG

☐ Please send me a giant-sized double-sided collectors' poster.
AND ☐ I enclose 6 tokens and have taped a £1 coin to the other side of this page.

☐ Please send me ☐ Mr. Men Library case(s) and/or ☐ Little Miss library case(s) at £5.99 each inc P&P

☐ I enclose a cheque/postal order payable to Egmont UK Limited for £.............

OR ☐ Please debit my MasterCard / Visa / Maestro / Delta account (delete as appropriate) for £.............

Card no. ☐☐☐☐ ☐☐☐☐ ☐☐☐☐ ☐☐☐☐ ☐☐☐☐   Security code ☐☐☐

Issue no. (if available) ☐   Start Date ☐☐/☐☐/☐☐   Expiry Date ☐☐/☐☐/☐☐

Fan's name: ....   Date of birth: ....

Address: ....

....

Postcode: ....

Name of parent / guardian: ....

Email for parent / guardian: ....

Signature of parent / guardian: ....

Please allow 28 days for delivery. Offer is only available while stocks last. We reserve the right to change the terms of this offer at any time and we offer a 14 day money back guarantee. This does not affect your statutory rights. Offers apply to UK only.

☐ We may occasionally wish to send you information about other Egmont children's books.
If you would rather we didn't, please tick this box.   **Ref: LIM 001**